P9-BJH-783

CHIP 'N' DALE'S
Book of Seasons

By Cindy West
Illustrated by Paul Edwards

A GOLDEN BOOK • NEW YORK
Western Publishing Company, Inc., Racine, Wisconsin 53404

It was springtime! As the air grew warm in the friendly spring sun, all the trees began to bud and bluebirds sang happy new songs. But Donald Duck was so busy working, he hardly had time to notice.

"Spring is the time for planting," Donald reminded himself. "The seeds I plant now will grow into delicious vegetables this summer."

While Donald was busy digging, Chip and Dale were waking from their long winter's sleep. Chipmunks always sleep through the cold, snowy weather. But when the days are warm again, they wake up, eager to explore—and to eat!

"I'm hungry," Chip told Dale. "Look! Donald's digging up breakfast for us!"

Chip and Dale tiptoed over to Donald
Duck and picked up the acorns he'd dug
up with his shovel.

"You two are really lucky," Donald said with a sigh. "It's so easy for you to find food. But if I want to eat, I have to grow my own!"

As the days passed and the sun grew warmer, spring turned into summer. Baby birds hatched out of their eggs and the grass grew taller and taller. But Donald Duck was still working hard.

While Donald busily mowed his lawn Chip and Dale lay in his hammock, chewing dandelions.

"Don't these guys *ever* work?" Donald
wondered as he flipped them out of his
hammock.

"It's hard work to *rest* when Donald's
around," Chip complained.

Later on in the summer the tomatoes had grown round and red and the bees were busy making honey. Donald was busy, too. He was painting his picket fence.

"I know how to have some fun," Dale told Chip.

Chip and Dale sneaked into Donald's garden, where the ripe blackberries were fat and juicy. They gobbled up as many blackberries as they could, and then they put some berries in a bag.

Chip and Dale sneaked up to Donald's paint bucket and dropped the purple berries right in!

Donald was so busy daydreaming about going swimming that he kept brushing on the paint. When he finally saw his white fence turning purple, Donald blew his top! "One of these days I'll get even with those chipmunks!" he cried.

When autumn came, cool winds began
to blow. Chip and Dale lay high in their
tree, watching the colorful leaves falling
down.

As usual, Donald Duck was working very
hard, sawing hickory wood for the winter.

As Donald piled up the wood he smiled. "Those rascally chipmunks can't mess up my work this time."

But he was wrong! Chip and Dale were nosing around his woodpile, searching for acorns to store away for the winter.

"Oh, no!" Donald shouted as he watched his neat woodpile tumble down.

"They did it *again*!" Donald groaned.

When the winter snow began to fall, Donald said with a sigh, "This has been such a hard year! I haven't had a moment's rest. And now I've got to shovel snow!"

Later Donald saw some tiny footprints.
Chip and Dale had not yet gone to sleep
for the winter. They wanted one more day
of fun.

"Aha! I see Chip and Dale are up to their
old tricks," said Donald. "But this time *I'm*
going to trick *them*!"

Chip and Dale worked very hard, tugging and pushing Donald's sled to the top of the hill. Suddenly Donald Duck came up and grabbed it away. "Thanks for all the work, you guys! Now it's *my* turn to breeze along!"

And so, for the very first time all year, Donald really relaxed.

"I showed those chipmunks," Donald said, laughing. "They did the work and I'm having the fun."

Chip and Dale chuckled. "We fooled him again," they said as they rode happily down the hill.